No voy a dormir
I Am Not Going to Sleep

NO VOY A DORMIR/I AM NOT GOING TO SLEEP

12-09

8-

Library of Congress Cataloging-in-Publication Data

Gribel, Christiane.
  [Não vou dormir. English & Spanish]
  No voy a dormir / Christiane Gribel ; ilustrado por Orlando. I am not
going to sleep / Christiane Gribel ; illustrated by Orlando.
     p. cm.
  Summary: In bed with her teddy bear, a little girl tries unsuccessfully to
stay awake.
  ISBN 978-1-933032-51-1 (pbk.)
  [1. Bedtime--Fiction. 2. Sleep--Fiction. 3. Spanish language materials--
Bilingual.] I. Orlando, ill. II. Title. III. Title: I am not going to sleep.
  PZ73.G7154 2008
  [E]--dc22
                              2008024561

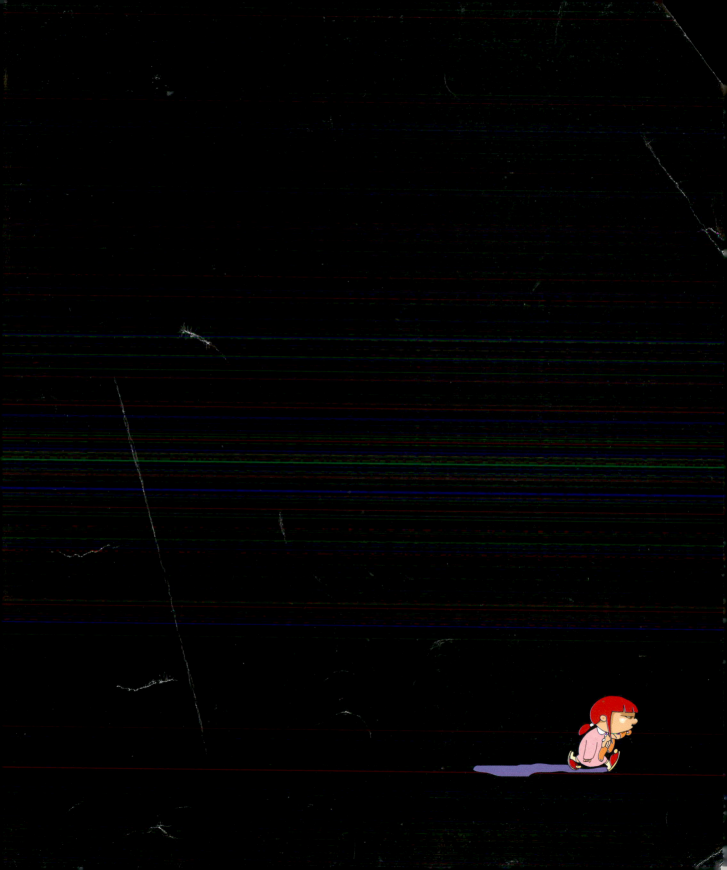

No voy a dormir
I Am Not Going to Sleep

Christiane Gribel
Ilustrado por/Illustrated by Orlando

LECTORUM
PUBLICATIONS INC.
a subsidiary of Scholastic Inc.
New York

–No voy a dormir –dijo la niña.
"I am not going to sleep," said the little girl.

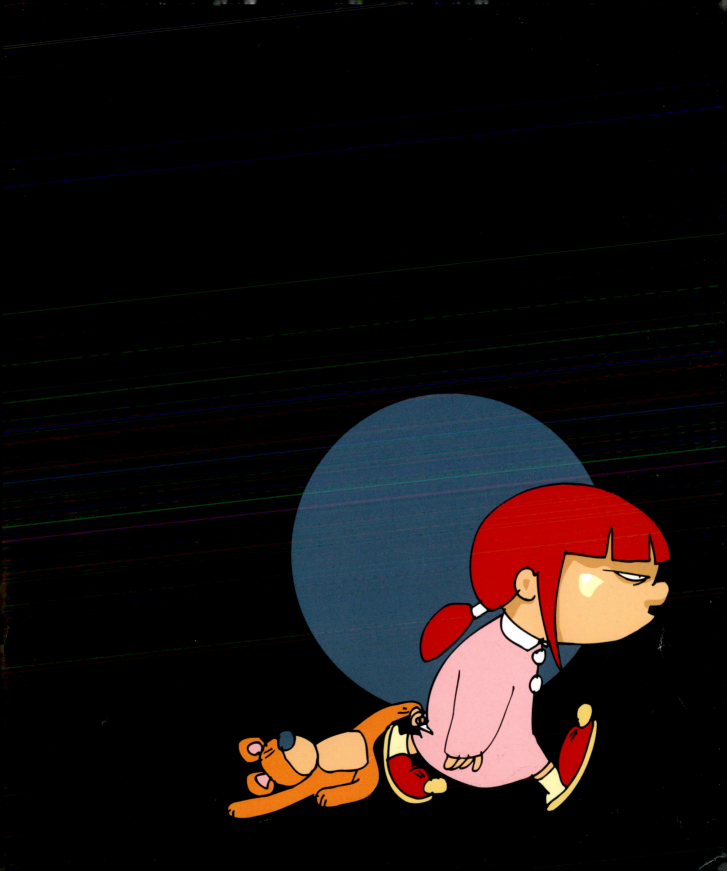

Me voy a quedar bien despierta en la cama.
I am going to stay wide awake in my bed.

No tengo sueño.
I am not sleepy.

Mamá me mandó a la cama.
Mommy sent me to bed.

Pero eso no quiere decir que me vaya a dormir.
But that doesn't mean I am going to sleep.

No me voy a dormir.
I am not going to sleep.

No tengo sue…ño.
I am not sleep…y.

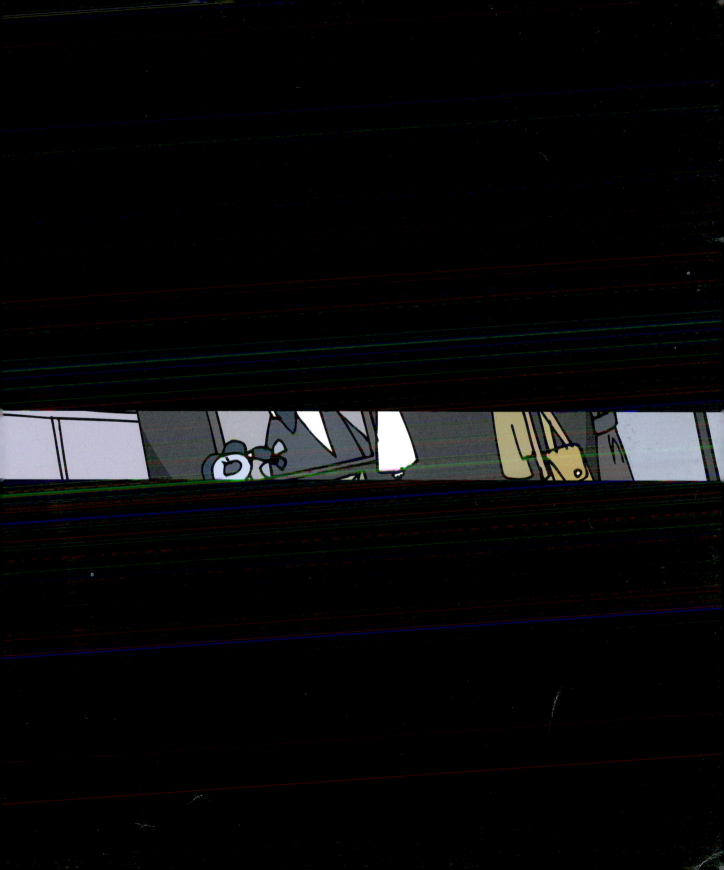

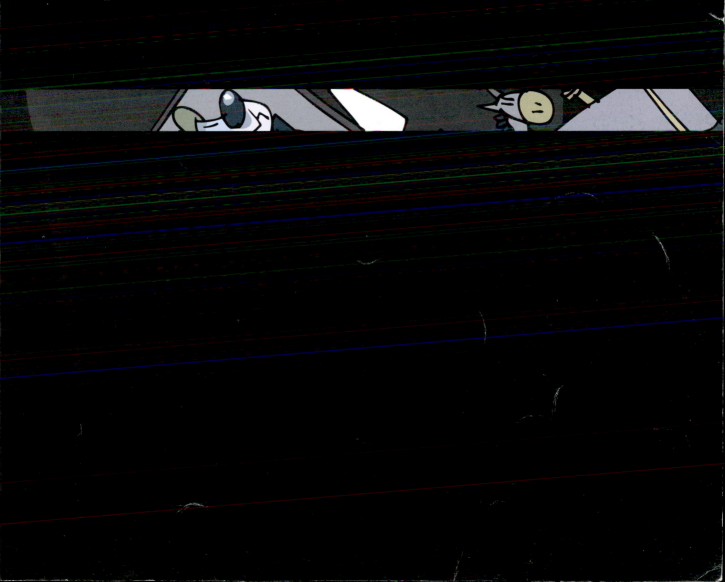

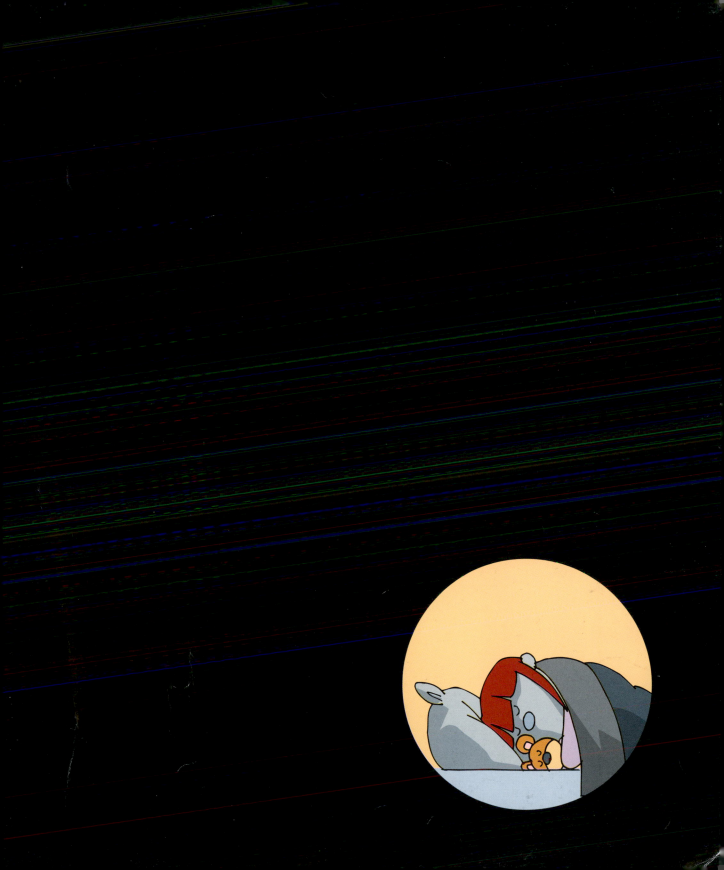

Christiane Gribel

Nací en Rio de Janeiro.

Vivía en una calle muy ruidosa, llena de autobuses y autos. Aun así yo dormía muy bien en mi cuarto que daba a esa calle. Luego me mudé a otro sitio y mi habitación daba a un gran bosque. Los grillos hacían aquel ruidito *cri-cri* toda la noche y yo me quedaba pensando en qué extraños animalitos podrían entrar por la ventana en cuanto hubiera cerrado los ojos de noche. Pero ningún animalito entró jamás y yo me acostumbré al cantar de los grillos. Ahora vivo en São Paulo y me he acostumbrado a vivir con el ruido de los aviones. Lo único que no consigo es acostumbrarme a dormir temprano. Miro el reloj toda la noche y pienso: "Ah, no me voy a dormir. Todavía no. Tengo tantas cosas que quiero hazzz…zzz…zzz".

I lived on a very busy street, full of buses and cars. However, I was able to sleep very well in my room facing the street. Later, I moved to another place and my bedroom faced a big forest. I could hear the sounds the crickets made all night long, and I would keep imagining all kinds of animals crawling through the window when I closed my eyes at night. But no animals ever crawled in and I got used to the sounds of the crickets. Now I live in São Paulo and have gotten used to the sound of the planes. I look at the clock all night and I think, "Ah, I am not going to sleep. Not yet. I still have lots of things to dooo…zzz…zzz."

Orlando Pedroso

Orlando Pedroso duerme poco. Nació en São Paulo en 1959. Ilustrador y artista gráfico, colabora con el periódico *Folha de S. Paulo* desde 1985 y también con grandes publicaciones y casas editoriales. Ha presidido jurados de diferentes premios de ilustración y ha sido premiado él mismo. Forma parte del consejo de la SIB (Sociedad de Ilustradores de Brasil). Le gusta dormir, pero odia tener que ir a la cama.

Orlando Pedroso doesn't sleep much. He was born in São Paulo in 1959. An illustrator and graphic artist, he has contributed to the newspaper *Folha de S. Paulo* since 1985 and has also worked with large publishing companies. He has served as a judge for many writing and illustration awards, and he has been the recipient of several awards himself. He is on the board of SIB (Society of Brazilian Illustrators). He likes to sleep, but hates going to bed.